A GIFT FOR SOPHIE

Story and Songs by Gilles Vigneault
Illustrated by Stéphane Jorisch

Sophie was seven years old and was as pretty as can be, with her two red braids that were always dancing on her head. She loved to draw. She would draw the house with all its windows and its big chimney on the eastern gable. She would draw her father, her mother, and her little brother also, who was only eight months old. But she also loved to draw her great-uncle Tom who everybody called "Old Man Tom."

He was very, very old and didn't have a hair on his head, but a long white beard. It was easier to draw. Old Man Tom never left his home, but at least it wasn't too far a walk. Sophie would go there almost every day. And each time, she would bring him a new drawing. And each time, her uncle had a little present for her. The first time, it was a small book with a single tiny sentence written inside. Another time, it was a little ring or a small bracelet, an old picture of him when he was young and a thousand other knick-knacks that had as only value the fact that they were given with love and for pleasure. He would often say of Sophie's drawings:

"My sweet Sophie, there is nothing more precious you could give me!"

Sophie also had a friend called Emilio who had, according to her, skin the color of caramel. Sophie liked caramel a lot. She also liked Emilio a lot. She loved to draw him because it would add color to her pictures.

I forgot to add she had a big black cat with spots she called "Sir" whose favorite sport was bird hunting. She could warn and threaten him all she wanted… but it was in the nature of things.
Oh, well.

They all lived in a tiny village near a huge lake. Every morning, Emilio, whose father fished all manner of pike and perch, would go and try his luck on a beach near his house.

On a beautiful April morning, Emilio came back home, quite excited. He'd seen something on the beach that had shone right through the sand. It was a large piece of rather thick glass that seemed to have in it every color there ever was. The sun had a part to play in this, of course… but this large jewel seemed magic to Emilio… full of mystery. And the colors shone right through the glass to dress the walls and furniture with its light.

"Now that's the perfect gift for Sophie!"

And he left straight away to surprise her with his treasure. Sophie was delighted! They played all day with the piece of broken glass that had been the bottom of a heavy bottle. But Emilio waited until nightfall before giving it to Sophie. She put it under her pillow to sleep.

The next day, quick-quickly, she went to see Old Man Tom to show him Emilio's gift: he was quite impressed. He went on to explain the prism and told her how it broke down light, which, in the eyes of Sophie, made Emilio's gift even more valuable.

She called it "The Eye."

Days and months passed. Many pictures were drawn with all the colors of the Eye and the sun. Autumn came. The leaves fell from the trees, and the old uncle fell sick. Emilio and Sophie's last visit, at the end of October, was filled with sadness, despite all the efforts Old Man Tom made to laugh with them and lighten the mood. In the end, he told them:

"If you ever come across a problem that you need my help to solve… call upon me… even if I'm gone! I'll ask the Good Lord's permission to come to your help…"

He died shortly after. Which caused great sadness to everyone… But just as Old Man Tom would often say:

"It's all in the nature of things!"

And it is in the nature of children to go on, to forget all sadness and… to live! Winter came and went, with its snowmen and its toboggans, with its skating and skiing and walks through the small woods, imagining yourself a hunter… And Spring came again, with the crow telling one and all:

"Caw… caw… caw…"

On her windowsill, Sophie kept every single present that Old Man Tom had given her, but her favorite was without a doubt the Eye of every color. Every morning, the sun would create a new rainbow on her ceiling. Yet on a beautiful morning in April, she had a very unpleasant surprise… she couldn't see the familiar rainbow stain on her ceiling. And looking at her windowsill, she saw that Emilio's gift was gone. Yet she was certain that she'd put it right in its place the night before! What could have happened?

She asked her father, and he didn't know anything about it. Yet her mother told her:

"Well, last night, I opened your window so that you could have some fresh air, but I can't imagine anyone…"

Indeed, she couldn't imagine anyone would just up and take it. It was going to be hard to break the news to Emilio. Since he would find out eventually, Sophie decided to tell him everything and enlist his help.

Of course Emilio was disappointed, but excited nonetheless by the opportunity: after all, he could finally act like the detective he knew himself to be, and show his sleuthing skills. So, they started to think. Could it have been Sir? But what would a cat do with a piece of glass? Let's go see. Sir was quite surprised that anyone would accuse him of anything... he'd been in his basket all night after all, sleeping tight. They'd reached this point in their investigation when Emilio suddenly remembered:

"What if we asked Old Man Tom?"

He didn't dare finish his sentence.

"Old Man Tom died," Sophie said, soberly.

"But he told us that if ever…"

"It's true, that he'd help us… or that he'd ask permission to help us."

"Trying can't hurt. Things can't get worse."

"Okay, let's try… but how do we do it?"

"Well… I guess it's like praying. We don't say a word, close our eyes, and ask Old Man Tom to help us find the Eye."

And so, in the middle of the day, near the big maple tree that was starting to show its leaves, Sophie and Emilio closed their eyes and asked the Old Man… or perhaps his soul, to keep his promise.

After a few long minutes of silence, a silence loaded with memories, Emilio said:

"Ok… we've asked him. Now we have to wait."

They waited. Until nightfall. Nothing came to them. Well, we will see tomorrow. And maybe Old Man Tom is quite far away now. Where? God only knows. And so they fell asleep with that on their minds.

The next morning, very early, Sophie asked Emilio to come and see her as quickly as possible. Without wasting a moment, he rushed to Sophie's house.

"So, any news?"

"Yes, I dreamt… I dreamt that Sir spoke to me…"

"A cat that talks?"

"Yes, he was talking in my dream. I was accusing him of having sold my beautiful Eye, and he was saying: 'Me, Miss Sophie, I'm only interested in birds. And I never steal from anyone, not me! Speaking of birds why don't you go ask the crow about your pretty piece of glass… Who knows, maybe it will have heard something, hmm? Now go on before you start accusing the first animal to cross your path…' And then the cat just walked off, laughing."

"I got it," Emilio said, "I got it! One day, Old Man Tom told me that crows love anything that shines. Let's go examine its nest at the top of the maple tree."

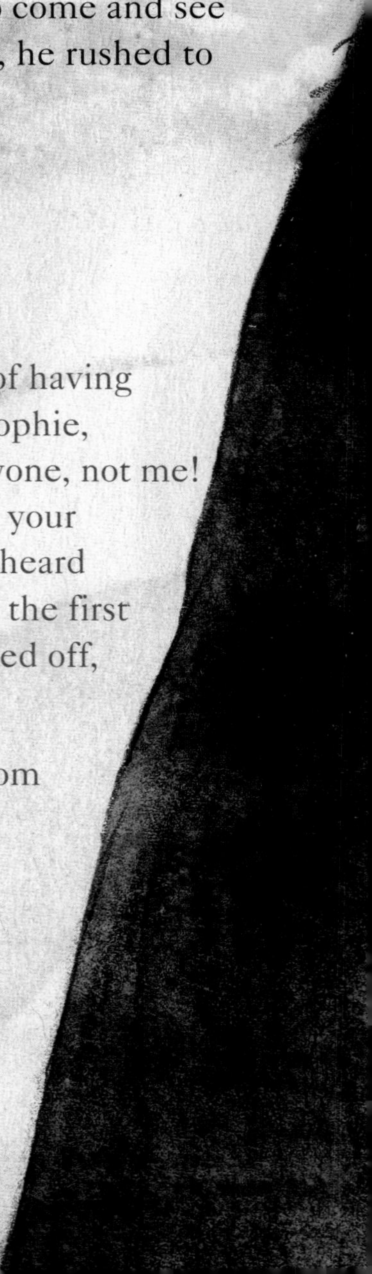

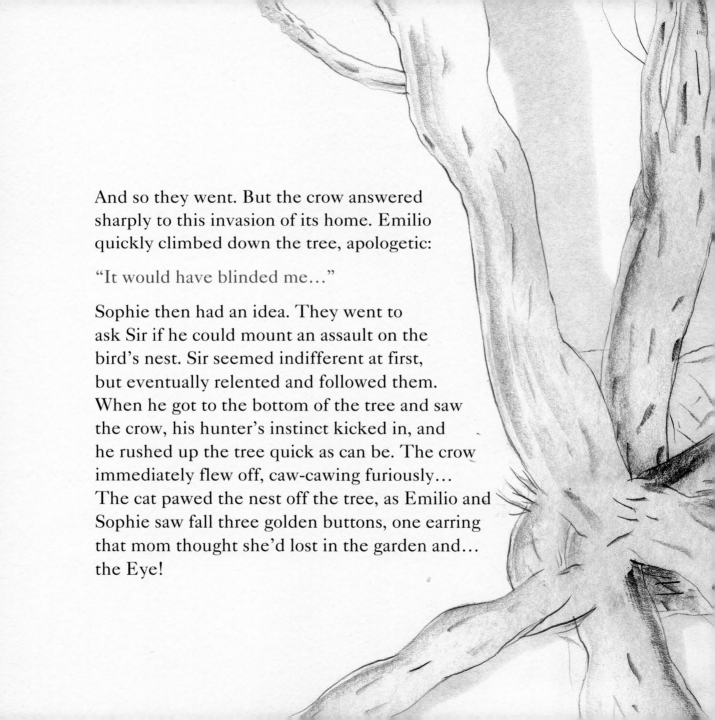

And so they went. But the crow answered sharply to this invasion of its home. Emilio quickly climbed down the tree, apologetic:

"It would have blinded me…"

Sophie then had an idea. They went to ask Sir if he could mount an assault on the bird's nest. Sir seemed indifferent at first, but eventually relented and followed them. When he got to the bottom of the tree and saw the crow, his hunter's instinct kicked in, and he rushed up the tree quick as can be. The crow immediately flew off, caw-cawing furiously… The cat pawed the nest off the tree, as Emilio and Sophie saw fall three golden buttons, one earring that mom thought she'd lost in the garden and… the Eye!

They had a big party, and even Sir was invited. A bowl of milk was poured in his honor, which he was happy to accept. The crow left and found itself a new home. Sophie's father built her a small jewelry box in which she put Emilio's precious gifts, every night, before going to bed.

And one night, as she was thinking of Old Man Tom, she opened
the first present he'd given to her, the tiny book with its tiny phrase.
And written in the tiniest of handwriting… Even in the most humble
present, we must see all the treasures of the heart.

A GIFT FOR SOPHIE

Story and Songs by Gilles Vigneault
Illustrated by Stéphane Jorisch

Lyrics

Nursery Rhyme for the Coming Times

LYRICS Gilles Vigneault AND Michelle Campagne | MUSIC Gilles Vigneault | SINGER Martin Léon AND Paul Campagne

Whatever your age
Your life's a blank page
Whatever you do
There's no one like you
Explore your own space
And you'll find your place
Explore your own rhyme
And you'll find the time

Your ancestors show
The way you must go
Through them you will see
That you hold the key
In your hand is drawn
The road that you're on
Only you can write
Your day and your night

If love begs your soul
To play a man's role
It's the wisest of aims
Of your childhood games
Love will fill your sails
Guide you on your trails
Shine your light upon
This planet you're on

In the galaxy
Where life came to be
Mysteries abound
Answers can be found
Open wide your eyes
Turn them to the skies
But never forget
The Earth under threat

Open wide your eyes
Turn them to the skies
Find the time to look
Inside every nook
Ring the morning bells
Sing of cockle shells
Songs for kids like you
From one to ninety-two

I've a New Friend (Sophie's Song)

LYRICS Gilles Vigneault AND Michelle Campagne | MUSIC Gilles Vigneault AND Bruno Fecteau | SINGER Martha Wainwright

I've a new friend and I like him
Being with him is a joy
And he never has a problem
For he's a boy

He's a prince upon a lakeshore
He befriends the escargots
He knows what lies on the seashore
Emilio

He's three apples high, no taller
Sweet as honey, you can tell
His complexion is the color
Of caramel

My Emilio is gorgeous
I could draw him every day
He says that I am mischievous
And runs away

Always By Her Side (Emilio's Song)

LYRICS Gilles Vigneault, Michelle Campagne AND Jessica Vigneault |
MUSIC Gilles Vigneault AND Bruno Fecteau | SINGER Thomas Hellman

Last spring on the fishing docks
I made a new friend
She is seven and she walks
Barefoot on the sand

I am always by her side
Finding on the shore
Treasures brought up by the tide
All for her and more

But whenever I don't understand her
I write her name in the sand with a feather

She has tons of nursery rhymes
Floating in her head
Which, for me, she'll sing sometimes
Or she'll draw instead

She has pretty eyes of green
She's a trickster too
The reddest hair you've ever seen
I like her, I do

But whenever I don't understand her
I write her name in the sand with a feather

It's All In the Nature of Things (Old Man Tom's Song)

LYRICS Gilles Vigneault AND Michelle Campagne |
MUSIC Gilles Vigneault AND Bruno Fecteau | SINGER Thomas Hellman

The sea offers to boys and girls
Some gifts that it hides in the sand
Some driftwood, some shells and some pearls
The sea and the wind, hand in hand
The wind, the wind
And the marvelous treasures it brings!
It's all in the nature of things

The cat is always on the chase
Hunting for prey on its own
The dog seeks forever the place
Where others have buried their bones
The bones, the bones
Feeding the flowers that grow in the spring
It's all in the nature of things

In the heart of every old man
A little boy plays a new game
The apple will fall from his hand
And give the apple tree its name
Its name, its name
Planting the seed of the song that he sings
It's all in the nature of things

A Hunter Through and Through (Sir's Song)

LYRICS Gilles Vigneault AND Michelle Campagne | MUSIC Gilles Vigneault AND Bruno Fecteau | SINGER Jessica Vigneault

Making life hard for the rat
Is in the nature of the cat
Mice and moles and then two thirds
Of most types of common birds
They will all confirm that torture
Is also in the nature
Of a cat

I have soft and fluffy fur
That is why they call me 'Sir'
With some patience and some time
You'll catch fowl for suppertime
It's in my nature to be rude
You see, I play with my food
It's fun!

I'm a hunter through and through
Naturally, it's what I do
I can't live on love alone
But on meat and fish and bone
And of course on sour cream
It's in my nature, it would seem
And you?

I Feather My Nest (The Crow's Song)

LYRICS Gilles Vigneault AND Michelle Campagne | MUSIC Gilles Vigneault AND Bruno Fecteau | SINGER Paul Campagne

I love all that shimmers
For I am the crow
I search for what glimmers
Wherever I go
The earrings that glitter
They whisper: 'Hello'
Caw... they whisper: 'Hello'

With trinkets and bangles
I feather my nest
My goal is to wrangle
The broach from your chest
Gold rings and fandangles
Nothing but the best
Caw...nothing but the best

The diamonds you're wearing
I think are divine
And since you're not sharing
I"ll just make them mine
I can't help my staring
I love things that shine
Caw...I love things that shine

With Just One Piece of Wood

LYRICS Gilles Vigneault AND Michelle Campagne |
MUSIC Gilles Vigneault AND Robert Bibeau | SINGER Jessica Vigneault

With just one piece of wood
And two pieces of string
Three nails
Four wails
The hammer on your thumb
Five curses, six bad words
Seven grommets from your boots
For grommets of the sail
Eight oclock
Heave ho!
Nine years old, the perfect age
To be a ship's first mate

And that was the very first boat

She was moored upon the reef
Next to the shore
With her anchor pulled tight
For the wind with all his might
Would have blown her away
And we lived our lives well

With nothing but one look
Two names carved in a tree
Three hearts
Four arrows
Tomorrow we will go
Five detours and six roads
My seven favorite marbles
I'm saving them for you
August eighth
Hair so red
Nine years old, the perfect age
To be a gallant knight

And that was the very first love

We had gone into the woods
To the blueberry patch
And we ate, we had our fill
And we stayed there until
The setting sun had disappeared
And we lived our lives well

With one too many word
Two angry silent days
Three times
Four times
She didn't meet me there
Five sighs and six tears
A tree with seven names
She won't come back to me
Eight o'clock
Too late!
Nine years old, the perfect age
To have a broken heart

And that was the very first heartache

With summer at an end
I'll count the days
For when school starts again
Once more I'll see my friend
I will gaze upon her face
And live my life well

With nary but one look
Two whispers in her ear
Three days
Four nights
We two in constant sight
Five departures, six returns
We've chosen seven names
I've made a room for you
Eight o'clock
Come on by
Nine months, the perfect time
To build a universe

And that was the very first child

He was and will always be
The only hope
He's a gift from above
He'll fall in and out of love
Somedays his heart will ache

And he'll build his first boat
With just one piece of wood
And two pieces of string

Old Tom's House

LYRICS Gilles Vigneault AND Michelle Campagne | MUSIC Gilles Vigneault AND Jessica Vigneault |
SINGERS Martha Wainwright, Thomas Hellman AND Jessica Vigneault

And when they returned
once more
To Old Tom's house on the hill
All was quiet, all was still
Much like it had been before

They went on without a word
Up to the top of the stairs
But there was nobody there
Only silence could be heard

As they'd done the last few years
Knocked three times, went
through the door
Found a paper on the floor
With these words:
'Hello my dears'

'Come to my house every day
In my suitcase you will find
Gifts for you of every kind
You must take the time to play'

Then came the discovery
Of a suitcase on the ground
And the two eight-year-olds found
A most wondrous legacy

And so then, for a full year
Sophie and Emilio
To Tom's house, went to and fro
Filling it with lively cheer

The Suitcase Waltz

LYRICS Gilles Vigneault AND Michelle Campagne | MUSIC Gilles Vigneault AND Jessica Vigneault |
SINGER Martha Wainwright, Thomas Hellman AND Jessica Vigneault

Seven wooden flutes
A little train that toots
And a tiny acorn
For Emilio
A game of dominos
And of tic-tac-toe

Multicolored string
And an Aztec ring
That's for Sophie dear
Postcards from Nepal
Seventeen in all
And a Russian doll

Seven silver bells
Abalone shells
Copper coins from China
A butterfly cocoon
Pictures of the moon
And a silver spoon

An ink pot and a quill
On the windowsill
From a bygone age
'Friendship has no price'
Written neat and nice
On a grain of rice

In a gospel book
Hiding in a nook
Was a pretty flower
Calming, sweet perfume
From the brittle bloom
Filled the tiny room

And a few short lines
From a book of rhymes
On the afterlife
'Cause it's good for you
A spot where you can brew
A pot of tea for two

Pining for the sun
A prism had been hung
Over by the window
Dancing in the light
Dazzling and bright
Seven hues alight

On a parchment page
Yellowing with age
Were the words: 'I love you'
I love you, I do
I'll come back to you
When you need me to

RECORD PRODUCER Paul Campagne ARTISTIC DIRECTOR Roland Stringer
PROJECT CONSULTANT Jessica Vigneault ILLUSTRATIONS Stéphane Jorisch
DESIGNER Stéphan Lorti FOR Haus Design RECORDED BY Paul Campagne AND Davy Gallant
at Studio King AND Dogger Pond Music MIXED AND MASTERED BY Davy Gallant at Dogger
Pond Music STORY TRANSLATION Jacob Homel COPY EDITOR Ruth Joseph

RECORDING OF THE STORY *A Gift for Sophie* David Francis NARRATOR | Mia Gallant SOPHIE
Toby Gallant EMILIO | Thomas Hellman THE CAT SIR | Jessica Vigneault SOPHIE'S MOTHER |
André Gallant OLD MAN TOM

MUSICIANS Paul Campagne ACOUSTIC AND ELECTRIC GUITAR, BASS, UPRIGHT BASS,
UKULELE Davy Gallant DRUMS, PERCUSSIONS, FLUTE, WHISTLE Jessica Vigneault PIANO
Steve Normandin ACCORDION Jonathan Moorman VIOLIN Yves Adam CLARINET
Martin Léon DRUMS, PERCUSSIONS, ACOUSTIC GUITAR (NURSERY RHYME FOR THE COMING
TIMES) Pierre Flynn PIANO (IT'S ALL IN THE NATURE OF THINGS)
Carl Naud ACOUSTIC AND ELECTRIC GUITAR (WITH JUST ONE PIECE OF WOOD)
Mia Gallant VOICE (FRÈRE JACQUES / RHYME FOR THE COMING TIMES)

Martha Wainwright APPEARS COURTESY OF MAPLEMUSIC, WARNER MUSIC AND CO-OPERATIVE
MUSIC Thomas Hellman APPEARS COURTESY OF SPECTRA MUSIQUE

THANK YOU TO Alison Foy-Vigneault, Karen Demeusy, Danny Goldberg, Wayne Rooks,
Bruno Robitaille, Jeffrey Gallant, Mona Cochingyan AND Connie Kaldor

Ⓦ www.thesecretmountain.com Ⓟ Ⓒ 2013 The Secret Mountain (Folle Avoine Productions)
ISBN-10: 2-923163-98-2 / ISBN-13: 978-2-923163-98-7